2 7 DEC 2018

D1138399

C555075283

Honesty Wart
Witch Hunter

Honesty Wart
Witch Hunter

Alan MacDonald

illustrations by Mark Beech

BLOOMSBURY

Ditherus Wart

Captain Custardly Wart

Sir Bigwart

Wart

Tyler Wart

Lord 'Bingo' Bottomley-Wart

Sharper Wart

Honesty Wart

The Wart family tree.....

First published in Great Britain in 2008 by Bloomsbury Publishing Plc
36 Soho Square, London, W1D 3QY

Text copyright © Alan MacDonald 2008
Illustrations copyright © Mark Beech 2008

The moral rights of the author and illustrator have been asserted

All rights reserved
No part of this publication may be reproduced or
transmitted by any means, electronic, mechanical, photocopying
or otherwise, without the prior permission of the publisher

A CIP catalogue record of this book is available from the British Library

ISBN 978 0 7475 9469 7

All papers used by Bloomsbury Publishing are natural, recyclable products made
from wood grown in well-managed forests. The manufacturing processes conform to
the environmental regulations of the country of origin.

Printed in Great Britain by Clays Ltd, St Ives Plc

1 3 5 7 9 10 8 6 4 2

www.bloomsbury.com

It's Behind You!

Foreword

by

Professor Frank Lee Barking (M.A. D. Phil)

Since the dawn of time members of the hapless Wart family have been dogged by disaster. From facing flesh-eating ogres to grappling with gladiators and being kidnapped by pirates, Warts have looked Death in the eye and lived to tell the tale. Now, thanks to years of painstaking research, and literally hours of daydreaming, I am proud to bring you the absolutely true and epic saga of . . .

The History of Warts

Chapter 1

Worry Wart

'For all your good and gracious gifts we thank thee, O Lord.'

'Amen,' said Honesty Wart, opening his eyes.

'Amen,' chorused his sisters, Mercy and Patience, whose prayers always went on longer than anyone else's.

Honesty's mum removed the lid of the dish on the table. Inside was a mess of dull brown splodge. It didn't look like meat, it looked like . . . well,

Honesty tried not to think what it looked like.

'Turnip mash,' said Mum. 'Pass your bowl.'

Honesty watched as she dolloped a spoonful into his bowl and banged it down in front of him. He stared at the splodge, watching the steam slowly rising from it.

'Something the matter?'

'No,' said Honesty. 'It looks . . . um . . . nice.'

'He doesn't like it,' said Mercy.

'I do!' said Honesty.

'He doesn't. We like it, don't we, Patience?'

'We like everything,' said Patience.

'I think turnip's delicious,' said Mercy.

Honesty glared at his two little sisters. In their dull grey dresses and white caps they looked like identical twins.

'Eat up, lad,' said Dad, giving him a friendly nudge. 'Turnip's good for you. Make you big and strong.'

'Better get used to it,' warned Mum. 'It's all you'll be getting for the next two weeks.'

'Why?' asked Honesty.

'Ask your father.'

'Why, Dad? Didn't you get paid again?'

''Course I got paid,' Dad replied, not looking at him. 'Just not in shillings and pence.'

'A sack of turnips!' Mum snorted. 'For two weeks' labour.'

'Not any old turnips,' said Dad. 'Samuels said they're the best turnips you'll ever taste. He was doing me a favour.'

Mum shook her head at him. 'You're a simpleton, William Wart. I should have seen that when I married you.'

Dad caught Honesty's eye and turned his mouth

down at the corners. Honesty tried not to laugh. His mum didn't approve of laughter. Not at the table, not in the house. There were a lot of things Mum didn't approve of. A verse hung on the wall to remind them of their Christian duty. It said:

'Let me do my work this day
Waste no time on fun and play,
Speak no ill and tell no lie,
Pray and toil until I die.'

Honesty felt depressed every time he looked at it. He chewed on his mashed turnip. It tasted disgusting. Two weeks of turnips for breakfast, lunch and dinner, he thought. Boiled turnip, stewed turnip, mashed turnip – he'd probably get turnip to take to school.

At least there was Christmas to look forward to. People in the village of Little Snorley didn't get excited about much. Most of them were Puritans like Honesty's family, so excitement was frowned upon. They read their Bible, said their prayers and went to church twice on the Sabbath. They didn't sing, dance or gamble, and kept away from ungodly places such as taverns or theatres. But Christmas was different. Christmas was the one day of the year when everyone in the village came together to celebrate. There would be a log blazing in the hearth and holly and ivy hanging from the rafters. Best of all, thought Honesty, there would be Christmas dinner: mince pies, plum pudding and, if he was lucky, a roast goose as big as a football.

'When are we getting the goose?' he asked.

Mum frowned at him. 'What?'

'For Christmas dinner. The goose.'

His mum and dad exchanged looks. 'Haven't you told them yet?' asked Mum.

Dad looked sheepish. 'I was going to. I just . . . well, haven't got round to it.'

Honesty could tell that bad news was coming. Even Mercy and Patience had stopped eating their supper. Had somebody died? Were they having boiled turnip for Christmas dinner?

'What?' he asked. 'Tell us what?'

'Honesty, lad.' Dad laid a hand gently on his shoulder. 'Don't take it too hard, but well . . . there isn't going to be any Christmas this year.'

'No . . . Christmas?' Honesty thought his dad must

be joking, except Mum didn't approve of jokes.

Mum pursed her lips. 'Parliament passed a law. Christmas is banned – and a good thing too if you ask me.'

'But we always have Christmas! It's the best day of the year! The only day we're allowed to have fun!' Honesty knew he was raising his voice, but he couldn't help it.

His mother glared and pointed her spoon at him. 'Fun? Playing at cards and dice? You call that fun? Drinking and brawling in the streets?'

'But Mum, we don't do any of that,' protested Honesty.

'We don't but that won't stop other folk. In London I hear they go to the theatre on Christmas Day. Some of the actors are *women*!' Mum gave a shudder.

Dad shook his head sadly. 'Surely it can't do any harm to give the children a little present, Agnes.'

'I don't mind not getting a present,' said Mercy nobly.

'No,' said Patience. 'It's better to give than to receive.'

'Presents?' said Mum, going red in the face. 'You

sit there and talk about presents when all we have to
eat is *turnip*?'

'I know,' said Dad, 'but –'

'What does it say in Scripture? "Go to thy work,
thou sluggard."'

'What's a sluggard?' asked Patience.

'It's a very big slug,' answered Mercy.

Honesty tried to get back to the point. 'But Mum,
if we don't have Christmas, what will we do all day?'

'The same as we do any other day,' snapped Mum.
'We'll work and pray and go to bed. Now, are you
eating that turnip or letting it go cold?'

Honesty ate the rest of his meal in silence. Never in his life had he felt so utterly miserable. He was used to disappointment but he had been looking forward to Christmas for weeks and weeks, crossing off the days on the calendar. Now 25th December would be like any other day of the year – deathly dull. Life couldn't get any worse. Or so he thought.

'Honesty,' said his mum, 'take some supper up to your gran.'

Chapter 2

Granny Wart

Honesty slowly climbed the stairs to his gran's room, taking care not to drop the bowl of lukewarm turnip mash. He stood on the landing, summoning his nerve. The truth was, he wasn't sure if Gran was quite right in the head. She was a bit odd. In fact there were times when she gave him the creeps.

'Gran, it's me! I've brought your supper!' he called.

The door creaked open when he pushed it. There was no sign of Gran. He stepped into the dark, stale-smelling room and set down the bowl of food on a pile of books. He had never understood why Gran got a bedroom all to herself. The house only had two rooms but Honesty had to sleep downstairs with his mum, dad and sisters.

And why did Gran clutter her room with so many strange things – things that he didn't like to look at too closely? Every shelf was piled high with objects, books and papers. There was a red toadstool growing in a jar. Dozens of other glass jars and bottles jostled for space on the shelves. He peered inside at bits of bone, cobwebs and frogspawn. There were tiny bottles containing cloudy liquids of every colour. A candle on the mantelpiece gave out a dim light but never seemed to burn any lower. Dusty books and charts covered the floor, piled high on top of each other. On one pile a pair of yellow eyes snapped open and blinked at him.

'CROOOARRRK!'

Honesty jumped backwards in surprise. It was Gran's pet toad, Merlin.

'See anything that interests you?' Honesty spun

10

round to find Gran sitting in her high-backed chair. She must have been there all the time, watching him. He suspected she did this kind of thing deliberately. Sometimes he wondered if she appeared out of thin air – you could never be sure with Gran.

'Did he frighten you, my sweet?'

'No, no,' said Honesty. 'I just didn't see him.'

Gran scooped up Merlin in her hand. 'I was talking to him, not you,' she said. 'There, there, my sweetheart, don't you worry. I won't let him harm you.'

This was another strange thing about Gran. She talked to Merlin as if he could understand every word.

'I brought your supper,' said Honesty, keen to get away as soon as possible. 'It's got a bit cold.'

Gran sniffed the brown mush. 'What's this meant to be?'

'Turnip.'

'Blech! Where's my mutton broth? I always have broth.'

'It's turnip tonight, Gran. Try it.'

'Don't talk rubbish! Put it down, boy, before you drop it.'

Honesty did as he was told. He watched his grandmother as she stroked Merlin's horny back. Her skin was as wrinkled as tree bark, hanging in great pouches under her eyes. Her grey hair hung over her shoulders in tangles and knots. Her nose was hooked like a hawk's beak, which made him feel she might peck him if he got too close. Honesty didn't know how old she was, but at a guess he would have said one hundred and sixty.

'Come closer, where I can see you better.' She beckoned with a long fingernail.

Honesty edged towards the door. 'I can't stay long, Gran. I think Dad needs me downstairs.'

'Rubbish! Stay a minute and talk to your old gran. Come here.'

Gran was smiling at him – a thin, crafty smile showing her three yellow teeth – two on the bottom, one on the top. She had a moustache too and curly white hairs sprouting from a mole on her chin.

'What's the matter? Something's upset you, hasn't it? I can see.'

'No, I'm fine,' said Honesty. Another disturbing thing about Gran was the way she could read your mind. It was whispered in the village she had second sight. Honesty wasn't exactly sure what this meant, but he was pretty sure it wasn't normal.

'Come now, you can tell your gran. What's the trouble, my dear?' she crooned.

Honesty took a step forward. Gran's hand snaked out and seized his wrist, pulling him close. For an old woman she had a surprisingly strong grip.

'Ow! You're hurting, Gran!'

'There now. I won't bite. Tell your gran all about it.'

Honesty sighed. 'You know it's Christmas in three weeks?'

'What of it?'

'Mum says it's banned this year.'

'Banned? What do you mean, boy? We always have Christmas.'

Honesty explained what his mum had said about the law Parliament had passed. Gran cackled with laughter. 'Ban Christmas? The fools! They might as well try and ban dancing.'

'They have,' said Honesty.

'Since when?'

'Since last year. You can go to prison for dancing.'

'The world's gone mad.' Gran shook her head. She still had hold of his wrist. 'And this is what's troubling you, is it? You'll miss your Christmas dinner?'

Honesty nodded glumly. 'We were going to have goose,' he said. 'Dad promised. And mince pies and plum pudding.'

'Then have them we will. Who's going to stop us, I'd like to know?'

'But it's the law, Gran! Mum says Christmas will be just like any other day.'

'Don't you listen to your mother,' said Gran. 'Listen to me. If I say we'll have Christmas, then we will.'

'But how, Gran?' asked Honesty.

'You leave it to me. I have my ways.' Gran's finger tapped the side of her bony old nose. 'There's things you know nothing about. Things they don't teach you at school.'

'What kind of things?' asked Honesty.

Gran's eyes widened. 'Secret things.'

'Anyway,' Honesty said, backing towards the door, 'thanks for the chat, but I ought to be getting back.'

Gran's bright little eyes flashed at him. 'Not so fast. I haven't finished yet. You want my help, then you'll have to do something in return.'

'What?' asked Honesty.

Merlin had crawled up Gran's chest and was now squatting on top of her head. It looked like she was wearing an ugly brown bonnet.

'Oh, you'll see. Nothing difficult. I can't get about like I used to, not with my poor old legs.'

Honesty weighed it up. He should have guessed his gran was up to something.

'Christmas dinner,' she said, smacking her lips together. 'Best meal of the year. Think of that fat roast goose. I like a leg myself, a nice juicy leg . . .'

Honesty's mouth was watering. 'All right!' he cried. 'I'll do it. As long as it's nothing . . . you know . . .'

'What?'

'Magic.'

Gran narrowed her eyes at him. 'Magic? Who said anything about magic?'

Chapter 3

Night Visitors

Honesty lay awake. The midnight chimes of the church clock were striking. He could hear his little sisters breathing from beyond the curtain that divided the room. His dad was snoring as usual.

It's not as if I'm doing anything wrong, he told himself. *I haven't told a lie. I'm only helping Gran*. Honesty had a dread of telling lies, probably because of his name.

Gran had said that the visitors would arrive before

midnight. She hadn't told him who they were. All he had to do was show them upstairs without waking anyone else. All the same he felt guilty: his mum said he should never let strangers into the house. And why were Gran's friends coming in the middle of the night? Were they robbers? Murderers? Even worse, witches? What if they were looking for small boys who would fit nicely in a cooking pot?

Plunk! Plunk!

He held his breath. Someone was throwing pebbles against the window. The witches were here already. He pulled his blanket over his head, hoping they'd go away.

Plunk! Plunk! CRACK!

If they carried on like this, they'd smash the window and wake the whole house. Taking the candle from the mantelpiece, Honesty stole to the door in his bare feet. His hand was trembling as he drew back the bolt and opened the door an inch.

It took a few moments to make out their faces in the dark. He was relieved to see two neighbours from the village: Ratty Annie and old Tom Turner.

'Let us in,' hissed Ratty Annie. 'We're freezing to death.'

Honesty led them upstairs. He knocked softly on Gran's door and after a moment it opened.

'You're late,' grumbled Gran. 'Close the door behind you.'

With the four of them inside, the little room was crowded. Tom Turner had to duck his bald head to avoid thumping it on the ceiling. Gran settled herself in her high-backed chair and stared at her visitors.

'Well, what have you brought me?'

Ratty Annie stepped forward. She was a dirty-faced girl a few years older than Honesty. She fumbled in her pockets, bringing out two brown eggs

and something she held up by its tail. A rat. 'Brought you a nice big 'un. Caught him fresh this morning,' she said.

Her dad was the village rat catcher and she sold the dead rats for a farthing each. That was why everyone called her Ratty Annie.

'Thanks, but you keep it,' said Gran. 'I'll just take the eggs.'

'Sure?' said Ratty Annie. 'I'll save him for later then. Make a nice rat stew for Dad's supper tomorrow.' She slipped the rat back into her pocket.

Tom Turner had brought a gift of five green apples. 'I had six,' he explained, 'but I got hungry on the way. Saved you the apple core though.'

'Thoughtful of you,' said Gran. She put the eggs and the apples into a bowl.

'So, you want my help?'

Ratty Annie lowered her voice. 'They say you have powers. The second sight.'

Gran was stroking Merlin in her lap.

'They say lots of things,' she said. 'What is it you want?'

Ratty Annie chewed on a lock of her hair and looked at the ground. 'There's a boy.'

'Ahhh, a boy.' Gran nodded.

'I see him in church every Sunday. He sits across the aisle. But he never pays me no attention. Except once he caught me staring and called me a ratty old fleabag.' She glanced at Honesty, daring him to laugh. 'I want . . . him . . .'

'To like you?' smiled Gran.

'Why shouldn't he?' demanded Ratty Annie, glaring furiously. 'I'm as good as the rest, ain't I?'

'No one said you're not.'

'My dad reckons I'm pretty as a plum.' She twirled a lock of dirty hair round her finger and glanced at Honesty. 'You laugh and I'll land you one.'

'I'm not laughing,' said Honesty, trying to look serious. He had never imagined that Ratty Annie could be in love. Harder still was imagining anyone falling in love with her – keeping dead rats in your pockets wasn't exactly romantic.

'This boy. What's his name?' asked Gran.

'Jem,' answered Ratty Annie.

'Jem? Jem Swelter?' said Honesty.

'You know him? Isn't he the handsomest boy in the world?'

'Er . . . well . . .' This was hard to answer without

a barefaced lie. Big, mean, ugly: these were words that came to mind when Honesty thought of Swelter. Jem was the blacksmith's son, and he could pull rusty nails out of wood with his teeth. Honesty kept out of his way as much as possible.

'So you want this boy to fall in love with you?' Gran was saying.

Ratty Annie nodded. 'Can you do it?'

Gran put her head on one side. 'Leave it to me. We'll have him following you around like a dog.' She turned to her other visitor. 'And what about you, Tom Turner? Who are you in love with?'

'Me? No one. I'm married,' said Tom Turner. 'I keep bees.'

'Yes, so I've heard.'

'Bees is clever,' said Tom, lowering his voice as if this was a secret. 'Bees make honey.' Honesty had a feeling this was going to take some time.

'I can sell honey for three pence a pot, see? Three pence a pot,' said Tom.

'That's good, but I don't need any honey,' replied Gran.

'I can't sell you any, not if you beg me on your knees.'

'Why not?'

"Cos I don't have any.'

Honesty groaned. They'd get more sense out of a boiled potato.

'Listen,' said Gran. 'It's late, Tom. Why do you need my help?'

'I tried everything but they don't come out,' said Tom.

'The bees?'

'No. They stay in their hive and don't make a sound. I tried singing to them, but I don't know what kind of songs they like.'

'Anything they can hum along to,' suggested Honesty. Gran shot him a look.

Tom went on. 'My wife says to me, "Go and see old Granny Wart. She's clever. She'll know what to do." So I did. And here I am.'

Gran got to her feet suddenly, turfing Merlin on to the floor. 'Thank you, that's all I need to know. Now I expect you'll both want to be getting home.'

'But I brought you eggs!' said Ratty Annie. 'You haven't said what you're going to do!'

'Patience, child, patience,' said Gran. 'I'll send word to you both tomorrow along with something that will solve your problem. Honesty can bring it.'

'Me? Why me?' said Honesty.

Gran ignored him and showed her visitors out. Honesty took them downstairs and unbolted the front door. Luckily the sound of Dad's snoring still rumbled on.

When he returned, Gran was bent over the pages of one of her ancient books.

'Here we are. A potion for the lovesick,' she said.

'Anyone in love with Swelter *must* be sick,' remarked Honesty.

Gran muttered to herself as she traced the words on the page with her finger. Honesty peered over her shoulder.

'That's not a book of spells, is it?' he asked nervously.

'Don't talk nonsense!' Gran scribbled something

on a scrap of paper and handed it to him. 'These are the things I'm going to need.'

Honesty looked at the list, trying to read Gran's scratchy handwriting.

' "Juice of whale"?' he said.

'Snail,' said Gran. 'Juice of snail.'

'It sounds revolting. "Wing of bat"? Where am I going to find all this stuff?'

'You'll find it,' said Gran. 'Use your head.'

'And what about "True Love's Hair"? What does that mean?'

'What it says,' replied Gran, sitting down. 'If you're making a love potion, you need a hair of the beloved.'

Honesty let this sink in for a moment. 'You don't mean Swelter? You want me to ask him for a lock of his hair?'

'Of course not! Asking him will only make him suspicious. You'll have to get the hair without him knowing.'

'But how am I going to do that?'

Gran shrugged. 'You'll think of something.'

Honesty stared at the scrap of paper in his hand. He didn't think Gran realised what she was asking.

26

Snail juice was one thing, but stealing a hair from Jem Swelter's head? He might as well ask a bull if he could borrow the ring from its nose. And that wasn't the only thing that worried him either.

'What if Mum finds out?' he asked. 'She says magic is a bomination.'

Gran clicked her tongue. 'You're talking nonsense again. Who said anything about magic?'

'You did! You're making a love potion!'

'I'm helping people. Isn't that my Christian duty?'

'Well, yes, but –'

'There you are then. Now, off you go – it's late and I want to go to bed. Put it in your pocket and don't lose it. And remember, not a word to anyone.'

Honesty nodded. Who would he tell anyway? Certainly not his sisters (who couldn't keep a secret for ten seconds), and definitely not his mum (who would never believe him). He folded Gran's list in half and put it in his pocket. It had been a strange night. Tomorrow was going to be even worse.

Chapter 4

A Hairy Moment

Honesty unwrapped his hanky and inspected the disgusting things he'd collected so far. Why couldn't his gran be like other grandmothers? he wondered. Why did he have the kind of gran who sent you out looking for bat's wings and frogspawn?

It hadn't been easy finding the things on the list. He had found some snails under a rock on his way home from school and managed to coax two on to his hanky with a twig. Honesty had no idea how you extracted their 'juice'. Gran could do that bit herself. The bat's wing he'd found in a dark cave high above the village. It was still attached to a tiny dead bat. Ratty Annie had supplied him with the tail of a rat, although she'd had the nerve to charge him a farthing. The other things on the list he'd managed to find, but there was still one item he was putting off as long as possible: a hair from Jem Swelter's head.

The blacksmith's forge stood at the end of a muddy track that crossed a cow field. Honesty dawdled along it, hands in pockets, trying to ignore the sick feeling in the pit of his stomach. Talking to Swelter always brought him out in a sweat. He tried to think of a clever plan, but his mind was a blank. All he could picture was Swelter's ugly face and small, piggy eyes. He didn't attend school like other kids his age and no one tried to make him. He preferred to work at the forge with his dad, learning how to bludgeon things with a hammer.

He had reached a muddy yard at the end of the track. A horrible smell came from a pile of steaming cow dung in the corner. From inside the forge came a sound of bashing and hammering. Swelter and his father were at work. A large painted sign over the door read: **Jon Swelter and Sun – Blaksmifs** (spelling wasn't the Swelters' strong point).

Honesty crept up to the doorway and peeped inside. Jem Swelter was bent over a red-hot bra-

zier, holding something in the fire. Luckily there was no sign of his dad. Hanging on the walls were rows of black tools that looked like instruments of torture. Swelter was busy with his work and hadn't heard him approach. His thick brown hair hung over the back of his collar. (Honesty's hair was cut short because his mum said long hair was vanity.) He crept into the shadowy forge. The brazier made the room hot as a furnace. If he could only get within reach! He'd spotted a loose hair sticking up on the back of Swelter's head.

Swelter pulled out a glowing poker from the fire and began to wallop it with a hammer. CLANG! CLANG! CLANG!

Honesty was almost close enough to reach out and tap him on the shoulder. It was now or never. His hand was shaking as his fingers closed on the loose hair and tugged hard.

'EEEOWW!' It turned out it wasn't as loose as it looked.

Swelter swung round, red-faced and snorting. Honesty thought of an angry bull about to charge.

'You!'

'Oh ... er ... hello, Swelter,' said Honesty.

31

'You pulled my hair.'

'No, no, I didn't,' said Honesty. (This was a lie and Honesty tried not to tell lies but there was no time to feel guilty.)

'Why are you skulking round here?'

'I wasn't. I just dropped by to . . . you know . . . see how a blacksmith works. Is that a poker?'

Swelter was advancing on him with the hammer in one hand and a poker in the other. The tip was still glowing red. Honesty pointed at it nervously.

'You should be careful with that. It looks hot.'

'*Burning* hot,' said Swelter.

'You could hurt someone.' Honesty swallowed hard. He had backed out of the open door and into the bright light of the stinking yard. Swelter looked at the poker as if deciding what to do with it. A smile spread slowly across his ugly face. He cut the air with the poker as if it was a sword. Honesty had to leap backwards to avoid it.

'Careful!'

'What are you doing here?' demanded Swelter, jabbing the poker at his chest.

'Nothing. I told you, I just dropped by!'

'Liar!'

'I can explain . . .'

They had come to a stop. Honesty tried to think. His mum was always warning him to tell the truth. The truth never hurt anyone.

'I just wanted . . . I needed . . . um . . . a lock of your hair.'

'A what?'

Swelter narrowed his piggy eyes, trying to work out if Honesty was mocking him.

'Just one hair. A small one. If you could spare it. Please.'

'Think you're funny, do you?'

'No! I just need a hair. Not for me, for someone else. She . . . er . . . collects hair, especially nice brown hair like yours.' He was gabbling but for a moment it seemed to be working because Swelter dropped the poker in the dust. His hands balled into big fists. Honesty backed across the yard, trying to get away. His boots were sinking in some kind of mound, forcing him to stumble backwards uphill. Swelter gave a crooked grin and suddenly shoved him violently in the chest. Honesty fell backwards, landing on the hill with a damp squelch. It was the dung heap.

'HUR! HUR! HUR!' Swelter stood over him, braying like a donkey.

Honesty sat up with a sucking noise. His trousers clung to his bottom damply. There was something cold and wet stuck to his hair. He wiped it off and saw the brown mess on his fingers. Swelter was still doubled up with laughter.

'Hur! Hur! You fell in the dung heap! Hur hur!'

'JEM!' His father's voice rang out from the forge. 'Jem! Where in blazes are you?'

Jem's grin melted instantly and he scuttled back inside.

Honesty got to his feet, shaking the muck off his boots. It was time to go home.

As he turned to leave, something caught his eye. The door at the side of the forge was open and hanging from it was a jacket grimy with dirt and grease. Inside the forge he could hear Swelter getting a lecture from his dad. Slowly and without a sound, Honesty lifted down the jacket. Two or three hairs were stuck to the collar – brown hairs like Swelter's. Honesty picked one off and carefully wrapped it inside his hanky. Then he splodged off across the field, running as fast as he could. He prayed that he

could make it home without bumping into anyone
from school.

Chapter 5

The Whiff of Trouble

Naturally his mum went up the wall. She went on and on, asking him the pointless questions parents always ask. What was he thinking of? How did he manage it? Hadn't she told him a hundred times? Honesty had to stand in the yard shivering, while she threw buckets of freezing cold water over him. After that, she scrubbed him down with soap and a scrubbing brush that was sharp as needles. Even then the smell didn't go, it lingered on him like wood smoke. It would be months before anyone sat next to him at school again.

Mum thumped down a pot on the table and began to dish out supper.

'Your favourite. Turnip stew,' she said, pushing a bowl at Honesty.

The stew was heavily laced with salt in order to take away the taste of the turnips. Now it tasted mainly salty. Still, he knew better than to grumble.

'Well, you'll never guess what happened today,' said Dad, trying to lighten the mood.

'Don't slurp, Honesty,' scolded Mum.

'I didn't!'

'You did,' said Mercy. 'I heard you. Slurp, slurp, slurp.'

'It's rude to slurp,' said Patience.

Dad tried again. 'So anyway, coming home I ran into Ned Lumsden. He'd just got back from the market at Crowsfoot –' He broke off and sniffed the air. 'Can you smell something?'

'It's Honesty,' said Mercy.

'He smells,' said Patience, holding her nose.

Dad leaned closer and sniffed. 'Phooo! What happened to you?'

Honesty rolled his eyes. 'It's nothing. I had an accident.'

'He fell in a pile of cow's . . .' Mum couldn't bring herself to say the word.

'A pile of cows?' said Dad. 'What were they doing in a pile?'

'No! Cow's you-know-what.'

Dad still looked baffled. Honesty sank his head in his hands.

'*Cow poo*, all right? I fell in a pile of cow poo.'

His mum looked shocked. 'I won't have such language at the table!'

'Sorry! I only said cow –'

'Say that word again and you'll be going without supper!'

Honesty chased the stew around his bowl with a hunk of stale brown bread.

'Anyway,' said Dad, giving him a friendly nudge, 'what was I saying?'

'Something about Ned Lumsden,' said Mum.

'Oh, that's right. Ned Lumsden. You'll never guess what.'

'Just tell us,' groaned Mum.

'Well, they caught . . .' Dad paused dramatically. 'They caught *a witch*.'

'No!' said Mum.

'Yes.'

'In Crowsfoot?'

'That's what Ned told me.'

Honesty laid down his spoon, suddenly losing his appetite. 'Who is she?'

'Well, I didn't catch a name but she's a witch, right enough. The Witchfinder says so.'

'Witchfinder?' said Mum. 'What are you talking about?'

'The Witchfinder General. Didn't you hear? He rides from village to village on a black horse, finding witches. That's why they call him –'

'Yes, yes, the Witchfinder General,' said Mum. She sat back in her chair and clicked her tongue. 'It's an evil world we live in, a wicked, evil world. I hope you're listening to this, young Honesty.'

'Me? Why me?'

'Look at you. Stinking of cow's . . . business. Who knows what you've been up to?'

'I haven't done anything!' said Honesty. 'I just went for a walk.'

His cheeks were glowing. Once you got started, lying wasn't so difficult. Soon he wouldn't be able to stop. He stared at his bowl, stirring the lumps in his stew.

Mercy and Patience were full of questions. They wanted to know what the witch was like and whether she wore a black hat and rode in a pumpkin coach with rats for coachmen. Honesty thought they were getting confused with Cinderella.

'But what'll happen to her?' asked Honesty.

Dad wiped his mouth with his hand. 'She'll be hanged, I expect,' he replied. 'That's what they do with witches.'

'Serves her right,' scowled Mum. 'Wicked old hag.'

Honesty suddenly pushed back his chair and got to his feet.

'Where are you off to now?' Mum demanded.

'I thought I'd – um – just go and see Gran.'

'Sit down! You haven't finished your meal.'

Honesty sat down. All of a sudden he didn't feel well. It was almost too much to take in. A witch in Crowsfoot! Worse than that, a man on a black horse who could look into your soul and tell if you were a witch.

'Dad,' he said, 'this witch-catcher, he won't come here, will he?'

'I don't see why. He'd be wasting his time. There's no witches round here.'

'No,' said Honesty, glancing at the stairs.

'Why?' demanded Mum.

'No reason. I was just thinking . . . of Gran.'

His parents both stared at him.

'Gran? What's she got to do with it?'

'Nothing. Just . . . haven't you ever thought she's a bit strange?'

'Bless you, boy, she's old,' chuckled Dad. 'Of course she's got a few odd habits!'

'But all those things she keeps in her room,' said Honesty.

'Old people are like that,' said Mum. 'They get fond of things.'

'Toads,' said Mercy unexpectedly.

'Pardon?'

'Gran's fond of toads. She keeps one in her pocket. He's called Merlin.'

Patience nodded. 'I've heard her talking to him.'

'Anyway,' said Mum, clearing away the bowls, 'she's very good for her age. You'd be surprised what she knows. Now, if you've finished you can take up her supper.'

Honesty sighed and did as he was told. He wondered what his parents would say if he told them his Gran had visitors after midnight and was busy mixing a love potion for Ratty Annie. They probably wouldn't believe him.

'Shut the door!' snapped Gran when Honesty went up to see her.

'I've brought your supper, Gran.'

'Is it more of that turnip muck?'

'Yes.'

'You can feed it to the pigs.' She was sitting with her back towards him, stirring a black cooking pot that was warming over the fire. Steam rose up the narrow chimney. Honesty went closer to look. Inside the pot a dark liquid the colour of seaweed was swirling and bubbling like a swamp.

'Did you get everything I told you?' demanded Gran.

Honesty set down the bowl of stew and fished out his hanky. He unfolded it, showing her all the ingredients he'd collected.

'I left the snail in its shell,' he explained. 'I wasn't sure how to get the juice.'

Gran took the snail from him, set it on the floor and walloped it with a heavy book. CRUNCH!

'Snail juice,' she said, showing him the sticky mess stuck to the book cover. She scraped it into the pot along with the bits of shell. Honesty felt he was going to be sick.

Gran wrinkled her nose, sniffing him.

'What have you been up to? Jumping in cowpats?'

'It's a long story,' sighed Honesty. 'I ran into a problem.'

Gran regarded him shrewdly. 'The blacksmith's boy eh? You should stand up to him. Don't let him push you around.'

'I don't!' Honesty sat down on a three-legged stool. 'Anyway, he's ten times my size.'

'Size isn't what counts. It's what you keep up here.' Gran tapped her head.

'My hair?'

'Your brain, you numbskull! Your brain.'

Honesty didn't answer. He couldn't see how using your brain could help against Jem Swelter. It wasn't as if you could challenge him to a spelling contest.

'How did you come by this then?' Gran picked up the long strand of Swelter's hair, holding it between her thumb and finger. Honesty explained how he'd spotted the hair on the collar of Swelter's jacket.

Gran nodded, showing her three yellow teeth. 'See? You used your head. Maybe you're not such a dullard.' She dropped the hair into the cauldron and they watched it swirl round and round with the bits of snail-shell. Gran began to stir the pot, crooning some kind of weird song to herself. It made the hairs stand up on the back of Honesty's neck.

> *Juice of nail and wing of bat,*
> *True love's hair and tail of rat,*
> *He who drinks this loving potion*
> *Pierce his heart with sweet devotion.'*

'There, that should do the trick,' said Gran.

'You think it will work?' asked Honesty. 'He'll actually fall in love with her?'

'You'll see. Drink this and he'll fall down and kiss her feet.'

'Eugh!' said Honesty. Personally, he'd rather kiss a skunk's bottom.

'But Gran,' he said, 'aren't you forgetting something? How are you going to make him drink it?'

Gran gave him a look. 'I'm not,' she said. 'You are.'

Honesty held up his hands. 'Oh no. I've done my part. I got everything you asked for. I'm not doing any more.'

Gran scooped up Merlin from the floor and placed him in her lap.

'As you wish. You won't be wanting that present then.'

Honesty stared. 'What present?'

'The one I was going to give you for Christmas.'

'You've got me a present?' Honesty hardly ever got any presents. His parents couldn't afford them. Even on his birthday all he got was a second-hand book called *Prayers and Hymns for Glad Occasions*.

'Well,' said Gran, 'it doesn't matter anyway. There isn't going to be any Christmas.'

'But Gran, you promised!'

'Only if you helped me – that was the bargain.'

Honesty sighed heavily. 'All right, what do I have to do?'

'Good boy,' said Gran. 'Come over here.' She fetched a small bottle and dipped it in the cooking pot, filling it with dark green liquid. A cork went into the top. From the pocket of her dress, she produced a second bottle of the same size. 'Two potions,' she said. 'Now, listen carefully. The green one is the love potion. Take it to Ratty Annie tomorrow and tell her the boy must drink it down, every drop. Got that?'

Honesty nodded. 'The green one for Ratty Annie.'

Gran held up the second bottle. The potion inside was golden brown.

'This one's for Tom Turner and his bees. Whatever you do, don't lose them.'

'I won't, Gran,' promised Honesty. 'Look, I'll keep them in different pockets so I know which is which.'

He tucked the bottles away, one in each of his

jacket pockets. Gran made him go over her instructions several times, just to be sure.

As he was going to the door, he remembered the conversation at supper and turned back.

'Gran, there's a man at Crowsfoot who can tell if you're a witch.'

'And why should that matter to me?' said Gran.

'Well, Dad was telling us at supper. If they prove you're a witch, they hang you.'

Gran didn't seem to be listening. Her head was tilted back in her chair and her eyes were closing. Merlin had nestled back in her lap.

Honesty crept out of the room, closing the door gently behind him. The voice made him jump.

'AND TELL YOUR MOTHER TO BRING ME SOME BROTH!'

Chapter 6

In the Soup

Ratty Annie's house sat high above the valley all by itself. The climb up the hill was one that would have tested a mountain goat. Honesty paused to sit down on a rock and catch his breath. For once he was confident nothing could go wrong. All he had to do was deliver the two potions, then life would return to normal and he could start looking forward to Christmas. He dug into his pocket and took out one of the potion bottles to examine it.

In the morning sunlight the dark green liquid shone like the sea.

He was so lost in his thoughts, he didn't notice the dark shadow fall across him. The man was mounted on a horse and gazing down at him from under a wide-brimmed hat. His hair was straight and black as a Bible, framing his sharp face like a pair of curtains. He smiled a wintry smile that was all lips and no teeth.

'Good day to you, my young friend!'

'Oh – good day!' Honesty jumped up and hastily stuffed the bottle back in his pocket. It clinked loudly against something.

'And what are you hiding there?'

'Where?'

'In your pocket.'

'Oh, that . . . um . . . nothing. Just water.' Honesty found the more you lied, the easier it got. At this rate he'd be an expert.

'Good,' said the stranger. 'I'm dying of thirst. Perhaps you can spare me a drop?'

He bent down from his horse, reaching out a hand.

'To – to drink?' stammered Honesty.

'If you'd be so kind.'

'You wouldn't want to drink this. It's . . . um . . . pond water. Look, it's all green.'

Honesty held up the seaweed-coloured potion to show him. The man seemed curious and took the bottle to examine it. He removed the cork and sniffed the contents. For one terrible moment Honesty thought he was going to tip back the bottle and drink the potion. He wished he would give it back.

'So tell me, my young friend, what's it for?'

'For?' repeated Honesty.

'This pond water you keep in your pocket.'

'Oh! er well . . .' Honesty racked his brains for an explanation. 'It's . . . for the ducks,' he said.

The man made an O shape with his mouth. 'The ducks??!'

'In the duck pond. Sometimes it dries up in winter, you see, so I always carry a little pond water in case they . . . um . . . need it.'

The stranger had evidently decided he was dealing with the village idiot. He handed back the bottle, which Honesty gratefully tucked away out of sight.

'I am Silas Brood. You've heard the name, no doubt?'

'Not really.'

'Oh. And what do they call you?'

'Honesty, sir.'

'A good name. Are you worthy of it? Do you always tell the truth?'

'Yes, sir, I try to.' Honesty checked to see if his nose had grown like Pinocchio's.

'You live round here?' asked Brood.

'Yes, sir.'

'Do you know of a village called Little Snoring?'

'Little Snorley. That's the church down there, in the valley.' Honesty pointed out the grey spire of St Wilfred's peeping above the trees.

'Thank you, Honesty. This is for you.'

The man took out a coin and pressed it into Honesty's hand.

'Thank you, sir.'

'Perhaps we'll meet again. I hope so. Good day to you.' Brood tipped his hat, dug in his heels and the black horse ambled off, following the zigzag track down the hill. Honesty watched him go. He inspected the coin in his hand: a penny. Silas Brood. It was a funny name, but he seemed a friendly sort.

Ratty Annie was waiting for him at the gate with her arms folded. Four or five skinny rats hung by their tails from the fence.

'Who was that?' she demanded.

'I don't know. But he gave me a penny.'

'What for?'

'I don't know.'

'You don't know much, do you?' said Ratty Annie scornfully.

Honesty grinned. 'I know you're in love with Jem Swelter.'

Ratty Annie thumped him hard on the arm.

'Ow! What was that for?' said Honesty.

'I felt like it,' replied Ratty Annie. 'Anyway, have you got it? She promised you'd bring it today.'

Honesty glanced over her shoulder to make sure no one was watching them from the house. He dug in his right pocket. It was empty. For one horrible moment he thought he'd lost the potion altogether. Then he checked in his other pocket and remembered he must have put it in there when he was talking to Silas Brood. He brought out both the potion bottles and showed them to Ratty Annie.

'Two?' she frowned. 'Why are there two?'

'One of them's for Tom Turner. I'm going on there next.'

'Which one is mine then?'

Honesty looked at the two bottles of potion in his hand. It dawned on him that he couldn't remember. Hadn't Gran said the green potion was for Ratty Annie? Or was it the golden-brown one? The more he thought about it, the less he was sure.

Ratty Annie pushed her face into his impatiently. 'I *said* which one is mine?'

'Oh! It's . . . ah . . . ' Honesty dithered. 'This one!' He plumped for the golden one and handed it over.

'You're sure?'

'Of course!' He was certain. Almost certain.

'What am I meant to do with it?' asked Ratty Annie.

'Just make sure Swelter drinks it – every drop or it won't work.'

'Leave it to me,' said Ratty Annie with a smile. She was already imagining Jem following her around with a lovestruck expression. Honesty left her by the gate, glad that at least he didn't have to face Swelter a second time.

By the time he reached old Tom Turner's cottage, the church clock had struck twelve. Turner was crouched over his beehive, looking through the hole where the bees came in and out. He was dressed in his bee-keeping outfit – an ancient straw hat with a piece of netting hanging over his face.

'Mr Turner?'

'Who's that?' Tom Turner peeled back the net and peered at him.

'It's me, sir. Honesty.'

'If it's honey you want, you're wasting your time. I haven't got any.'

'It's all right. My gran sent me,' said Honesty. 'She asked me to give you this.' He reached into his pocket and handed over the bottle.

'What's this?' asked Tom Turner.

'The potion you asked for.'

'Did I?'

'For the bees. Remember?'

Tom Turner beckoned him closer. 'I know they're in there, but they don't come out. I think they're hiding from me.' He pulled out the cork and sniffed the potion. 'What do I do with this?'

'I don't know,' said Honesty. 'They're supposed to drink it, I imagine.'

'Drink it?'

'Yes.'

Tom Turner shrugged, put the bottle to his lips

58

and gulped it down in one go before Honesty could stop him.

'Not bad,' he said, wiping his mouth with his hand. 'Could do with a little honey to sweeten it.'

Honesty stared at him open-mouthed.

'Um, Mr Turner?'

'Yes?'

'I think it was meant for the bees.'

'What?'

'The potion you just drank. It was for the bees.'

Tom Turner frowned. 'Well, why didn't you say so?'

'I did. You weren't listening.'

This wasn't going to plan. He watched Tom Turner closely for any signs of change in him. He half expected him to sprout a tiny pair of wings and zoom off into the air.

'How do you feel?' he asked.

'Fine.' The old man frowned at Honesty. 'What did you say your name was again?'

'Honesty.'

'Well, if it's honey you've come for, you're wasting your time. I haven't got any.'

Honesty decided it was time to go home. After

all, Gran had asked him to deliver two potions and that's exactly what he'd done. If things hadn't gone quite to plan, it couldn't be helped. In any case, it might be wiser not to say anything to Gran, he decided. At least if the potion did its work, Swelter would soon be hopelessly in love with Ratty Annie. That would be a sight worth seeing. Honesty climbed over a stile and back on to the main street, jumping over a muddy puddle. Coming in sight of his house, he stopped in his tracks. Standing in the yard was a large black horse.

Chapter 7

Witchfinder

Honesty found his family sitting around the table. His mum, dad and sisters were there along with the tall, sharp-faced stranger he'd encountered that morning. Silas Brood turned his head as he came in. His raven hair was swept back from his high forehead.

'You're late,' whispered Mercy.

'We've been waiting for *hours*,' added Patience.

'And the soup's getting cold,' said Mercy, sticking

out her tongue at him.

Honesty slid into the seat next to Dad, aware of Brood watching him closely. He wondered what the man was doing here.

Mum ladled watery turnip soup into six bowls. Honesty noticed that she'd set out the best cutlery, which usually only appeared on special occasions.

'This is Mr Brood,' she said. 'He's staying for dinner.'

'Oh, we've met before,' said Silas Brood, eyeing Honesty. 'The boy who looks after ducks.'

Honesty ignored his sisters' puzzled looks. It would take too long to explain.

'Turnip soup, Mr Brood?' offered Mum.

'You are kindness itself,' smiled Silas Brood.

'Patience, pass the salt to our guest.'

Brood held up a hand. 'Thank you, but I never take salt. Salt is the Devil's invention.'

'Is it?' asked Dad.

'I am a plain, simple man with simple tastes,' said Brood. 'A little soup, a morsel of bread – that is all I ask.' He smiled his wintry smile.

Mum quickly removed the salt and fetched the speckled brown loaf she'd baked for breakfast. Honesty watched hungrily as the guest cut himself a fat slice, leaving the crust to one side.

'Butter?' asked Mum.

'Thank you. I never take butter.'

Mum hastily removed the butter and hid it away in the cupboard. For a while there was only the sound of spoons scraping bowls. Honesty noticed that the guest had been given Mum's silver spoon, which normally no one was allowed to touch. It had belonged to her great-grandmother. Silas Brood helped himself to a second slice of bread and mopped up his soup. He seemed to have a good appetite.

'So what brings you to Little Snorley?' asked Dad.

'Ah, the Lord's work, brother.'

'You're in the church then? A parson?'

Brood's tongue located a crumb at the corner of his mouth. 'My calling is to seek the lost,' he said.

'Oh well, we all get lost,' said Dad. 'Only last week one of my pigs –'

'You misunderstand me,' Brood interrupted. 'I mean lost souls. Witches.'

Honesty dropped his spoon in his bowl, splattering his face with soup.

'Witches?' echoed Dad.

'Lord have mercy on us!' gasped Mum.

'Then you're that fellow everyone's talking about? The Witchfinder Corporal?' said Dad.

'Witchfinder General,' corrected Silas Brood. 'I had hoped to keep my identity a secret but I see my fame goes before me.'

Honesty could see his family were impressed. They'd never met anyone important before and a Witchfinder General sounded extremely important. Mum stood up and bobbed a curtsey as if she was meeting the Queen. Dad's eyes were bulging like a bullfrog's. Mercy and Patience were staring at the visitor as if he'd grown an extra head. Honesty, meanwhile, had turned pale and was trying not to panic. If the stranger sitting opposite him was the Witchfinder General, they were in major trouble. Gran was upstairs and the moment Brood set eyes on her he'd be able to tell she was a witch.

'Have you seen one?' asked Patience.

'A witch? Many times. Alas, in these evil times witches are everywhere.'

'But what do they look like?' asked Mercy.

Silas Brood raised a long pale finger. 'Ah, my child, that's their cunning. You might sit next to a witch at church on Sunday and never know it. Many of them look quite harmless, like your aunt or sister or grandmother. There might be one living in your village right now. Perhaps across the street. Even in this house where we are sitting this very moment, a witch could be listening.'

There was a silence so still you could have heard a cockroach breathing. Silas Brood sat back and smiled. 'The soup is delicious, by the way. Tell me, would this spoon be silver?'

'It was my great-grandmother's,' said Mum proudly.

'Really?'

'But if witches look like anybody else,' said Dad, anxious to get back to the subject, 'how do you know which is a witch and which isn't?'

Silas Brood clasped his bloodless hands together and lowered his voice. 'Believe me, brother, if there are witches in your village I will find them out. I will hunt them down like vermin.'

'*Plugh*!' Honesty spat a stringy lump of turnip into his bowl. Mum rolled her eyes.

'Sorry, it got stuck,' he croaked. 'Could I get down now, please?'

'Certainly not. Help me clear away these dirty plates.'

Honesty collected the bowls while their guest asked questions about the village. Did any of their neighbours have cats? Did any of them talk to themselves? Had anyone bought a cooking pot recently?

'Where are you staying, by the way?' asked Mum.

'I haven't decided,' replied Brood. 'I'm a simple man with simple needs. Anywhere will do.'

'There's the tavern,' suggested Dad. 'But it's six-

pence a night and the beds have fleas.'

Brood shook his head. 'Taverns are the Devil's lodgings. Perhaps there's a house in the village that would take in a poor weary traveller.'

Mum glanced at Dad. 'Well, you could always stay here.'

Honesty dropped one of the bowls on the table with a crash. Mum glanced at him sharply.

'Why not? He could sleep in Gran's room,' she said.

'But . . . but where would Gran go?' asked Honesty.

'Down here with us. It's only for a few nights.'

Silas Brood spread his pale hands. 'Please, you've been too kind already. I've no wish to put you to any trouble.'

'It's no trouble. It would be an honour to have you stay, wouldn't it, William?'

'A great honour,' agreed Dad.

Honesty groaned. This was turning into a bad dream. A witch hunter staying in their house, sleeping in Gran's room? Gran's room! He hadn't thought of that. Even if he could keep Gran out of sight, her room was cluttered with books and bottles and all the strange things she collected. They might as well hang a big sign on the door saying: 'WITCH'S LAIR – KEEP OUT!' He had to find an excuse to see Gran before their guest set eyes on her.

'Well, you must be tired from your journey,' Mum was saying. 'I expect you'd like to see your room and get unpacked.'

'NO!' yelped Honesty.

His mum looked at him. 'What do you mean "no"?'

'I mean ... um ... I wouldn't go up there yet.'

'Is something the matter?' asked Brood.

'It's just ... Gran might be sleeping,' gabbled Honesty. 'You know how old people sleep sometimes? So maybe I better go up and see if she's awake ...'

Before they could argue he had dashed up the stairs and was knocking on the door.

Chapter 8

Saving Gran

'Gran!' Honesty closed the door behind him and peered into the dim, smoky room. Gran was sitting in her high-backed chair by the fire, asleep. Honesty shook her by the arm.

'Gran, it's me! Wake up!'

Gran's eyes snapped open. 'What's all the noise? Can't I take a nap without you bothering me?'

'Sorry, but we've got to hurry.' Honesty was picking up armfuls of books from the floor. There was so much junk they'd need a hay-cart to shift it.

'What are you doing?' demanded Gran. 'What's going on?'

Honesty hardly knew where to start. He explained about the visitor and why he had come. Gran didn't sound in the least concerned.

'Witchfinder General?' she scoffed. 'Don't talk such nonsense!'

'It's true. He's downstairs, Gran, and he wants your room.'

'Tell him I'm using it.'

'I can't. Mum's already said he can sleep here for a few nights. That's why we've got to get rid of all this.'

Honesty had found a wooden box and began to load it up with jars, pots, bottles and books.

'Put those back!' Gran was starting to lose her temper.

'Gran, listen,' begged Honesty. 'If he sees any of this we're in terrible trouble.'

'He can mind his own business,' snapped Gran.

Honesty held out a jar in front of her nose. 'Look – cobwebs! Why would anyone collect cobwebs? He'll think you're a witch, Gran!'

Gran narrowed her eyes. 'Rubbish!'

Honesty waved a hand at the contents of the room. 'Look at this place! You talk to toads! You've been selling magic potions to the neighbours!'

'Nonsense! Herbal remedies, that's all. Did you deliver them like I told you?'

Honesty hesitated. There wasn't time to explain now.

'Of course I delivered them.' (It wasn't a lie – he had.)

There was a loud knock at the door.

'Honesty? What are you doing in there?' It was his mum.

'Nothing! Just tidying up! I'm nearly done.'

Honesty looked around in desperation. There was far too much junk for one person to carry. He'd just have to take what he could and hope for the best. He cleared the shelves, sweeping armfuls of bottles into the box. A stopper came out, spilling something that smelled like Swelter's armpits on a hot day.

'You could try and help!' he grumbled.

Gran ignored him, plumping herself down in her high-backed chair. Merlin popped his head out of the pocket of her black dress.

'Don't worry, my sweet, we're not going anywhere,' she cooed, stroking his fat spotted belly.

'Please! We have to hurry!'

The knocking at the door resumed. Honesty tried one last time.

'Gran, you know what they do with witches. I'm trying to help you!'

'Then you can start by putting everything back where it belongs.'

Honesty gave up; he had done his best. All he could do was hide what he had in the box and hope that Gran had the sense to keep her mouth shut.

The knocking was now a banging. Trying not to spill the box, he pulled open the door. Outside stood Silas Brood, with Mum hovering behind him anxiously. The Witchfinder's eyes fell on the box in Honesty's hands.

'I thought I heard raised voices,' he said. 'Is anything the matter?'

'No, no,' said Honesty. 'I was just moving some of Gran's things downstairs.'

'Helpful of you,' said Silas, blocking his way so he couldn't get past. He picked up one of the glass jars and examined it. Little white grubs squirmed against the glass.

'Maggots,' he said. 'How unusual.'

'Ye-es,' said Honesty. 'Gran likes to um ... go fishing on a Friday.'

'And what's this?' Silas picked up a bottle and tipped the contents into his hand. 'The skin of a lizard, if I'm not mistaken.'

'She collects skins,' said Honesty. 'You know, sheepskin – goatskin, lizard skin . . .'

'Really?' Silas Brood pushed past him into the darkened room. His eyes swept over the books and charts on the floor, the black cooking pot over the fire and the wrinkled, wild-haired old lady stroking a toad in her lap. Merlin let out a croak like a belch.

'And who might you be?' demanded Gran.

'Forgive me, we haven't met. Silas Brood, Witch-finder General.' Brood swept off his black hat. 'I do hope I'm not disturbing you.'

The smoky room had suddenly grown hot and airless. Honesty felt dizzy. The Witchfinder and his gran seemed to be locked into some kind of staring match where neither of them would blink or look away. Whatever happened next, he thought, it wasn't going to be good.

Downstairs, someone banged on the front door. Moments later they came pounding up the stairs and burst into the room. It was Ratty Annie, red-faced and wild-eyed.

'It's Jem!' she panted. 'You'd better come quickly.'

'Perhaps I can be of service. Is something the matter?' asked Brood.

Honesty shook his head at Annie, trying to warn her, but it was no use.

'He's on the roof,' said Ratty Annie. 'I think he's gone stark raving mad!'

Chapter 9

A Bit of a Flap

Word had spread quickly through the village. By the time they arrived a large crowd, two cows and a dog had gathered. Nothing much ever happened in Little Snorley so a boy on a roof was a sight not to be missed. Silas Brood had ridden over on his horse while Gran had left the house for the first time in months, hobbling along with her walking stick and grumbling all the way. They pushed their way into the middle of the crowd, where all eyes were looking up. It was growing dark by now but they could see the shape of a figure crouched on the roof.

'What's he doing?' asked Mercy.

'Nothing at the moment,' replied Mum. 'I think he's deciding whether to jump.'

Patience tugged at her dad's jacket. 'Lift me up, Dad! I want to see the boy jump!'

Jem Swelter was certainly behaving strangely. He tottered to the edge of the roof and peered down at the crowd. Then he flapped his arms like a chicken attempting to take off.

'Jem! Be careful – you'll fall!' called Ratty Annie anxiously.

'Buzz, buzz, buzz!' grinned Swelter in reply.

'Jem!' called his dad. 'Don't be a fool – get down off there!'

Swelter didn't pay any attention. He was humming a song that he'd composed himself.

> *'Buzz , buzz , buzz, bumbly bee,*
> *Honey, honey, honey for my bumbly tea.'*

Silas Brood looked up. 'How long has he been like this?'

'I don't know, sir,' replied Swelter's dad. 'He was all right at breakfast. The next thing I know, he's climbed up there and won't come down.'

'Buzz, buzz, buzz, bumbly bee!' chanted Swelter.

The crowd drew back. If he kept flapping his arms like that, he was certainly going to lose his balance and fall.

*

Gran seized Honesty by the ear and dragged him to one side.

'What have you done?' she hissed.

'Ow! Nothing!'

'I thought you said you gave him the potion.'

'I did!' replied Honesty. 'More or less.'

'More or less? Either you did or you didn't!'

'I gave it to Ratty Annie. She said she'd make sure he drank it.'

Gran released his ear. It hurt.

'Which potion?' she demanded. 'Think carefully.'

Honesty avoided looking at her.

'The golden one. Probably.'

'You dozy dollop! You mixed them up, didn't you? He's taken the wrong one.'

'Shh, Gran! Someone will hear!' pleaded Honesty. He'd caught sight of Silas Brood on his horse, watching them over the heads of the crowd. But Gran was too angry to take any notice.

'Do you realise what you've done?' she fumed.

'It wasn't my fault! It was an accident.'

'Accident? He's drunk a bottle of a potion meant for bees!'

Honesty looked up at Swelter. That would

certainly explain why he kept buzzing and flapping his arms. Swelter thought he was a bumblebee. Any moment now he might try to launch himself off the roof, aiming for the nearest clump of lavender. And there was another thing. If Swelter had drunk the potion, then Honesty must have given Tom Turner the love potion. And that meant . . . he didn't even want to think what it meant. It all came of telling lies. From now on, he vowed, he would stick to the truth.

A gasp escaped the crowd. Swelter was standing at the edge of the roof. He wobbled on one leg like a clown on a tightrope.

'I told you!' said Patience. 'He's going to jump!'

Swelter jumped. Honesty covered his eyes, hardly able to watch. Swelter hurtled earthwards like a plane in a tailspin. There was a tremendous SPLAT! as he landed head-first in something soft. It was the big pile of cow dung in the yard.

'URGGHH!' People turned away in disgust.

'Jem! Jem! Are you all right?' Ratty Annie had rushed over. Swelter picked himself up. He looked like the Incredible Blob. Brown muck oozed down his face and clung to his clothes.

'Runny honey, honey,' he said, licking his face.

The crowd backed away from him in case he needed any help. Ratty Annie was offering Swelter her hanky. She spotted Honesty.

'This is all your fault!' she shouted.

'Mine?' said Honesty.

'What's he got to do with it?' demanded Swelter's dad.

'Buzz, buzz, buzz,' sang Swelter, flapping his arms and scattering cow poo like carpet bombs. Everyone began to talk at once, arguing and jabbing their fingers.

'SILENCE!' boomed a commanding voice.

It was Silas Brood. The crowd obediently fell silent. They didn't know the stranger with the severe black hair, but he was riding a horse and anyone who rode a horse was obviously important.

'Brothers and sisters,' Brood began, 'many of you will know my name. It is Silas Brood.'

The villagers looked at each other blankly.

'The Witchfinder General,' prompted Brood.

The crowd stared at him awestruck. None of them had ever seen a real witchfinder before. They felt honoured that such a famous figure should visit their humble village. Some of the men removed their hats as if they were in church.

'Perhaps you're asking yourselves what all this means?' said Brood.

The villagers nodded. They hadn't been asking, but they were now.

'Consider the evidence of your own eyes. A boy who imagines he can fly. Is that normal? Is it natural?'

Heads were shaken.

'No, my friends, and I'll tell you why – this boy has been cursed by WITCHCRAFT!'

'Witchcraft!' wailed a woman in the front row.

'Witchcraft!' the villagers murmured to each other. Silas Brood turned his attention to Ratty Annie.

'You, girl. What is your part in this? Confess!'

'Me?' said Ratty Annie. 'I didn't do nothing. It wasn't me that gave it to him.'

'Gave what to him?'

'The potion!'

'Ah, the truth is laid bare,' said Brood dramatically. 'What was this potion? Who gave it to you?'

Ratty Annie and pointed.

'*He did!*'

Every head turned in Honesty's direction. He gulped and cleared his throat. Maybe this was a good moment to start telling the truth – then again, maybe not.

'Well?' asked Brood. 'What do you have to say?'

'It wasn't . . . er . . . really a potion,' said Honesty. 'More like a medicine – for . . . tummy ache.'

'And who made this "medicine"?'

Ratty Annie pointed again. 'Her! She mixed it up in her black cauldron. Granny Wart!'

Silas Brood's eyes gleamed with triumph. He spread both his arms wide.

'Behold the Witch!' he cried.

'Witch! Witch! Witch!' chanted the crowd, who by now were wildly excited. This was better than the annual 75-a-side football match. Two of them seized Gran by the arms and dragged her off towards the magistrate's house. Silas Brood went with them, leading the procession on his horse. Honesty and his family stood open-mouthed, watching them go.

'Is Grandma a witch, Dad?' asked Mercy.

'Of course not,' said Dad.

'But is she going to prison?'

'I don't know, love.'

'If she does,' said Mercy, 'can me and Patience have her bedroom?'

Chapter 10

How to Spot a Witch

The courtroom was packed, with every seat taken and children sitting in the aisles. News of the witch trial had spread like wildfire through the whole county. People had come from miles around, bringing their sandwiches in case the trial dragged on past twelve. Peddlers did a brisk trade outside the court, selling lace hankies embroidered with '*I've seen the Witch of Snorley*'.

Honesty had a good view from his place in the

front row. Gran sat only a few feet away, facing the court. A ruddy-faced man wearing riding boots and a ridiculously large wig entered the room. Everyone stood up.

Gran turned her head and whispered, 'Who's the bigwig?'

'Judge Gruntley,' Honesty replied.

'Is he a fair man?'

'I don't know. People call him "Gallows Gruntley".'

'Thanks for telling me,' muttered Gran.

'Don't worry, Gran,' said Honesty. 'I'll defend you. They're calling me as a witness.'

'Oh, that's all right then.' Gran gave him a withering look.

Judge Gruntley settled himself into his seat and banged his gavel for silence.

'Is this the witch?' he grunted. The clerk looked up from scribbling in his book.

'That's what we're here to decide, Your Worship.'

'She looks like a witch to me,' snorted Gruntley. 'What's your name, Grandma?'

Gran returned his gaze scornfully. 'Margery Wart.'

Judge Gruntley rose to his feet and straightened his wig. 'Margery Wart,' he boomed, 'you are guilty of the crime of witchcraft. I sentence you –'

The clerk interrupted, trying to get his attention. There was a brief whispered exchange.

'What? Oh, very well, if we must,' sighed the Judge. 'We'll hear the evidence before I pronounce sentence. Who speaks against the witch – er . . . defendant?'

Brood got to his feet. 'I do, Your Worship. Silas Brood. You probably know the name.'

'Can't say I do,' snorted the Judge. 'Keep it short. I've got four more cases to hear and I want my lunch.'

Honesty was called as the first witness. He was wearing his best Sunday suit and his hair had been brushed so hard it stood on end like a pincushion. He glanced at Gran nervously. The clerk handed him a Bible and he swore to tell the whole truth.

'Honesty, is this woman your grandmother?' asked Silas Brood.

'Yes, sir,' replied Honesty. He hoped all the questions were going to be this easy.

'Has she ever confessed to you that she is a witch?'

Honesty shook his head. 'No, sir . . .' (Gran nodded at him approvingly.) 'Other people are always saying it but Gran doesn't.'

'Which people do you mean?'

'Lots of people. Half the village.' Gran rolled her eyes up to heaven.

'Tell me, does your grandmother keep any pets? A black cat, for instance?'

'No, sir,' replied Honesty. 'Only Merlin.'

'Merlin?'

'Her toad. She keeps him in her pocket where she can talk to him.'

Silas Brood turned to the packed courtroom.

'Mark that. She talks to a toad. A certain proof of a witch.'

He went on with his questions. 'She sleeps in the upstairs room. Have you been in that room, Honesty?'

'Yes, sir. Lots of times. I take her meals up to her.'

'And what have you seen in there?'

'My gran,' replied Honesty.

'Besides her. Are there books of spells and curses?'

'I don't know. She won't let me read them.'

'A witch's cauldron perhaps?'

'No. But she's got a cooking pot.'

'Think carefully now. Have you ever seen your grandmother making a potion?'

'Um . . .' Honesty wasn't sure how to answer. If he said 'yes' it would confirm that Gran was a witch, but if he said 'no' he would be breaking his oath on the Bible. The courtroom suddenly seemed too hot. The white collar of his jacket was too tight.

'Well?' prompted Brood. 'It's a simple question.'

'She did . . . make something,' stammered Honesty. 'Yes?'

'But I'm not sure what it was. It may have been a . . . er . . . pudding.'

Silas Brood came closer, uncomfortably close. 'Tell me, what was in this "pudding" you saw?'

'In it?' Honesty felt his cheeks were on fire.

'Yes, in it.'

'Er . . . just the usual puddingy things.'

'Name them.'

'Well, ah . . . snail juice, a bat's wing, a lock of hair – just ordinary things.'

'Ordinary things.' Brood nodded and turned to the Judge with a satisfied smile on his face. 'Thank you, that will be all, Your Worship.'

Honesty returned to his place, giving Gran a thumbs-up sign as he sat down. She had her head in her hands so she didn't notice.

Ratty Annie was the next to be called. She stood facing the courtroom, glaring defiantly.

'Do you know this woman?' asked the Witch-finder General.

'What if I do?'

'Answer the question.'

'She's Granny Wart. Everyone knows her,' said Ratty Annie.

'Did she ever promise to make you a witch's potion?'

'Yes, she did.'

'A love potion?'

'It might have been.'

'Tell me, who was it for?'

'That's my business,' replied Ratty Annie.

'Remember, your oath on the Bible,' said Brood sternly. 'Who was this love potion for?'

Ratty Annie bit her lip and turned a delicate pink. 'Jem Swelter,' she mumbled.

'Jem Swelter, the blacksmith's son. And when he drank this potion, this witch's brew, what happened? Did he fall in love with you?' asked Brood.

Ratty Annie shook her head. 'No, it sent him mad. He climbed on a roof and tried to fly.'

'It almost killed him?'

'Yes,' said Annie. 'If he hadn't landed in the dung-hill he'd have died.'

Silas Brood waited for the laughter to die down.

'Mark that,' he said. 'The witch's potion almost killed him.'

He paced up and down a few times just for effect. 'Tell me, Annie, in the last week has anyone brought you flowers?'

Ratty Annie blushed an even deeper pink. 'They might have.'

'Who? Jem Swelter?'

'No. Tom Turner.'

'And why is that?' asked Brood.

'Ask him,' snorted Annie. 'He reckons he's dying of love. Keeps saying he wants to marry me.'

'Doesn't he have a wife already?'

'I don't ask him to pester me!' blazed Ratty Annie. 'He's mad as the moon!'

'And when did this touching courtship begin?' asked Brood.

'The day after he drank that potion. The one she sent him.'

'She?'

'Her. *The witch*!' Ratty Annie pointed a finger at Gran. People shook their heads and whispered among themselves. Honesty had a feeling things weren't going too well.

Other witnesses were called but none of them spoke in Gran's defence. Jem Swelter jumped on to a table, telling the court that he was a buzz-buzz-bumbly-bee. Tom Turner's wife claimed that the witch had cast a spell over her husband. Other neighbours came forward to claim that Granny Wart had turned their milk sour or caused them to lose a tooth.

'I lost a brooch,' claimed Mary Finch. 'The witch stole it from my room!'

'She stole my candlestick!' cried a woman.

'My wedding ring has vanished.'

'She took my father's snuffbox!'

People were standing up all over the courtroom, pointing at Gran and blaming her for everything but the weather. Honesty couldn't understand it. Gran

had been locked in a prison cell for five days, so how had she managed to cause so much trouble?

Finally Silas Brood called for the 'witch' herself to give evidence. Gran got to her feet and leaned on her knobbly walking stick.

'You've heard the charges against you?' said Brood.

'Gossip and lies,' snapped Gran.

'Take care what you say.'

'You take care,' said Gran, showing her yellow teeth. 'Maybe I'll turn you into a spider.' Silas Brood took a step backwards.

'You don't deny then that you meddle in witchcraft?'

'I never said I did,' replied Gran, leaning on her stick. 'People can tell all the lies they want, but it doesn't prove anything.'

The Witchfinder General turned to his audience. Most of them were hanging on his every word, apart from Judge Gruntley who had dozed off to sleep.

'How can you tell a witch?' asked Brood. 'What are the signs?'

A woman in the third row raised her hand. 'Ooh,

I know. If you say "Good morning, Witch" and she answers you, "Good morning".'

'Indeed,' said Silas Brood. 'But there are better ways. Perhaps some of you have heard of the Three Tests of a Witch?'

No one had but they were eager to see them. This was more like it. Accusations were all very well but they were hoping to see the witch swivel her head back to front or turn into a monkey and run off with the Judge's wig.

Brood continued pacing up and down. 'Every witch,' he said, 'has a certain spot or lump on their flesh which is so tender they cannot bear it to be touched. I call this place the Devil's Spot.'

The spectators nodded, many of them fingering their necks to check for lumps.

Silas Brood bent over Gran to examine her. He inspected her face, arms and throat. Next he ordered her to take off her shoes and peered at her wrinkled feet.

'Ah, just as I thought,' he said.

'What?' said Gran.

'Right there,' said Brood. He produced a feather from his pocket and touched the sole of Gran's foot.

'HA! HAA! NO, PLEASE!' shrieked Gran, kicking her legs violently.

'Hark how she screams,' said Silas Brood. 'She can't bear to be touched. A certain proof of a witch.'

Honesty turned to his dad. 'That's not fair,' he said. 'He tickled her feet!'

Silas Brood continued his 'examination'.

'The Second Test can be performed with a toad. I happen to have one with me.' He reached into his bag and brought out a fat brown toad with bulging eyes, holding it up for all to see.

'Merlin!' said Gran.

'A toad knows a witch by her smell,' said Brood. 'Watch how he goes to her.'

He set Merlin down on the floor. The toad didn't move. Brood gave him a sharp prod with the toe of his boot and Merlin set off, hopping across the courtroom. In three short leaps he had reached Gran's feet.

'There, there, my sweet, don't you fret. I've got you,' soothed Gran, picking him up.

'WITCH!' hissed someone near the front.

'Witch! Witch! Witch!' The whisper passed from one to another, growing in volume. Judge Gruntley woke up with a start and banged his hammer.

'Silence!' he bellowed. 'Margery Wart, I find you guilty of witchcraft. You will be taken to a place of execution –'

'No!' cried Honesty, leaping to his feet.

'Silence!' roared the Judge. 'Sit down!'

'But it's not fair!' Honesty protested. 'He said there were *three* tests. What about the third?'

Silas Brood raised a hand. 'If you will allow me to finish, Your Worship, the boy is quite correct. The third test is my personal favourite – the Swimming Test. The witch must be tried by water. She must be bound with strong ropes and thrown into a deep pond. If she floats, it proves she is a witch and she must be hanged. If she sinks, then it proves her innocence.'

Gran had turned pale. 'But I – I can't swim!' she croaked. 'I'll drown!'

'That,' said Silas Brood, 'is a risk we shall have to take.'

Chapter 11

That Sinking Feeling

Morning sunlight streamed through the front window, falling on Honesty's face. He blinked and yawned. He was sure there was something important he had to do today, some reason why he wanted to be up early. Slowly it came back to him. This morning was Gran's trial by water and he had to be there to save her.

Honesty struggled into his grey breeches, hopping around on one leg. Where were his shoes?

Where were the rest of his family? Normally Mercy and Patience were up by now, laying the table for breakfast.

There was no sign of them. Dirty plates and cups littered the table as if someone had left in a hurry. Honesty spotted a scrap of paper left under a bowl and snatched it up. It was a note written in his sister's childish scrawl.

> Bye lazybones. Gone to see Gran get wet.
> Mercy and Patience
> P.S. Your turn to wash up!

Unbelievable. They'd gone without him! He must have overslept and missed breakfast altogether.

Outside, the main street was deserted. Everyone seemed to have gone to watch Gran's ordeal. People had talked of nothing else for the past few days and no one wanted to miss the final act of the drama. Honesty glanced up at the church clock. Ten minutes to nine. If he ran all the way he could still get there in time. They would be at the pond at Flaxton Mill – the duck-pond in the village wasn't deep enough to drown a rat. He set off at a run, taking a short cut across the fields. *Please let me be in time*, he thought. *Please, please, please.*

Passing Tom Turner's house, he almost ran straight into a beehive. No buzzing came from the bell-shaped hive. When he peered through the hole, the bees didn't seem to be moving. They were either dead or asleep. *Of course!* thought Honesty. They were hibernating until the spring. No wonder old Tom Turner hadn't had any honey for months. An idea began to

take shape in Honesty's head. It wasn't the best idea he'd ever had but it was his only chance. Maybe the bees would help to prove Gran's innocence.

Meanwhile, at the millpond, Silas Brood was making final preparations. What he loved about the swimming test was the way it never failed. He had used it to test scores of witches and not one of them had survived. In his experience people wanted to see witches die a gruesome death. If there was lots of struggling, splashing and begging for mercy, so much the better.

A good crowd had turned out, gathered in a semicircle round one edge of the millpond. Brood had supervised the binding with ropes himself. The witch's right thumb was tied to her left big toe and her left thumb to her right big toe. It left her curled in a ball like a hedgehog – which guaranteed a good splash when they threw her in.

'Well then, witch, have you any last request?' asked Brood, loud enough for everyone to hear.

'The water looks nice. Perhaps you'd care to join me?' replied Gran.

'Very funny,' replied Brood. 'Pick her up.'

Two burly men stepped forward and carried Gran towards the water like a boat about to be launched. She turned her head to say a last word to her family.

'Tell Honesty I want him to look after Merlin. It's a pity he couldn't come to see me off.'

'He's still in bed,' said Mercy. 'But we're here, Gran.'

'We wouldn't have missed it for anything,' said Patience.

The men paused at the water's edge, waiting for the signal. The millpond looked deep and green and icy-cold.

'On the count of three, throw her in,' instructed Brood.

'Couldn't you make it a count of one?' pleaded one of the men. 'She's heavy!'

The villagers stood waiting. Gran was mumbling something under her breath that might have been a prayer or a spell. The Witchfinder General began the count.

'One, two, thr–'

'STOP!' yelled a voice. The crowd turned to see a boy tearing down the hill towards them, carrying a large beehive in his arms.

'Oh no!' groaned Mum. 'I might have known.'

'Wait!' panted Honesty. 'I've got something to…'
He was about to explain about the sleeping bees but
he was running so fast he didn't notice the millstone
in his path. He tripped and went sprawling headlong
in the mud, the beehive flying out of his arms. It
somersaulted through the air like an out-of-control

spacecraft and landed with a thud at the feet of Silas Brood.

'What's this?' asked the Witchfinder General, unwisely prodding the beehive with his toe. An angry drone came from inside, growing louder.

'Bzzz! Bzzzzzz! BZZZZZZZZZ!'

'Watch out!' cried Dad. 'BEES!'

The villagers scattered in every direction as the swarm rose from the hive in a black cloud. The two men holding Gran dumped her on the grass and took to their heels. Only Silas Brood was too slow to grasp the danger. The bees swarmed round him, buzzing in his ears.

'Argh! Yow! Heeeeeelp!' he howled, hopping and jigging around like a Morris Dancer. He staggered back blindly towards the millpond. For a moment he wobbled on the edge, then toppled backwards with a mighty SPLASH!

'Whoops!' said Honesty as the cloud of bees buzzed off into the grey sky.

The Witchfinder was thrashing around in the icy water.

'Blub, glub . . . I can't . . . glug!' he spluttered.

'Don't worry, he'll be all right,' said Dad. 'If he isn't a witch, he'll float.'

Mum shook her head. 'No, you daft donkey, it's the other way round. 'If he *is* a witch he'll float. If he isn't, he'll sink.'

They watched Silas Brood's head bob up once more, then disappear from sight.

'HEEELP! . . . UGGLE GLUG!'

'You're right, he *is* sinking,' said Dad.

Six or seven bubbles rose to the surface and burst one by one.

'Shouldn't someone dive in and save him or something?' asked Honesty.

Dad turned to the crowd and cleared his throat. 'Anyone here know how to swim?'

A minute later Silas Brood lay on the bank. His face was pale, his lips were blue and he was wearing a crown of pondweed. It was the blacksmith, John

Swelter, who had dived into the pond and dragged him out by the scruff of the neck.

'Is he dead?' asked Honesty.

'Don't be a fool,' said Gran, untying the ropes round her ankles. 'But if he doesn't change out of those wet clothes, he'll catch his death.'

Mum helped Brood struggle out of his wet clothes, trying not to look for the sake of decency. The Witchfinder huddled in a blanket, wearing only his undershirt and pants.

Honesty picked up his soggy coat, which made a jingling noise and was extremely heavy.

'What's he got in here?' he said.

'Don't touch that!' cried Silas Brood – but it was too late. Honesty had thrust his hand into the inside pocket and brought out a handful of shiny objects. He stared at them in astonishment.

'That's my great-grandmother's spoon!' said Mum indignantly.

'And my wedding ring!' said the woman next to her.

'My candlestick! My necklace!' cried others, crowding round.

Gran folded her arms and looked at them all.

'Well, I hope you're all proud of yourselves,' she scolded. 'Blaming a poor innocent old woman! As for this one,' she pointed at the wretched Brood. 'Witchfinder General? He wouldn't know a witch if one poked him in the eye with a wand! Ask him how he got all this.'

Brood confessed in sobs and gulps. It turned out that over the past week he had visited a dozen houses in the village. While he ate their bread and told them stories of his success, he kept an eye out for anything worth stealing.

'Want me to throw him back in?' offered the blacksmith.

'No,' said Gran. 'I think I've got a better idea.'

Ten minutes later Silas Brood was saddled on his black horse, wearing only his soggy underclothes and a pointed black hat on his head. A sign was pinned to his back which read: 'CHARLATAN' in big letters. The villagers of Little Snorley pursued him down the street, jeering and throwing rotten eggs.

'What does "charlatan" mean?' asked Patience as they tagged along at the back of the procession.

'It means big fat liar,' replied Mercy.

'Oh,' said Patience. 'We don't tell lies, do we, Mercy?'

'No, never,' said Mercy, smiling. 'Come on, let's run home. There might be some biscuits in the pot.'

Chapter 12

Gloomy Christmas!

Honesty watched the snowflakes splat on the windowpane and slide down. Two weeks had passed and it was finally here: 25th December, Christmas morning. He should have been jumping out of bed wild with excitement, but apart from the snow, there was nothing to look forward to. It was going to be the gloomiest Christmas ever. There would be no presents to open, no logs crackling in the fire, no carols to sing or visitors to welcome. Worst of all, they wouldn't be sitting down to Christmas dinner – his favourite meal of the whole year. Christmas was cancelled. Forbidden. Ever since Silas Brood had been chased from the village, Honesty had been hoping his gran might perform the miracle she'd promised. But, despite everything he'd done for her, she seemed to have forgotten. Today would be just like any other day of the year – deadly dull.

So he was surprised to see Gran dressed and sitting at the table. She had brushed her wild grey hair and even changed into her best black dress.

'Happy Christmas!' she greeted him.

Honesty's shoulders drooped. 'It's not happy – it's not even Christmas,' he moped. 'I might as well stay in bed.'

Gran glanced at the snow falling steadily outside the window. 'Cheer up,' she said. 'You never know what Christmas will bring.'

One by one, the rest of the family got up and sat down to a breakfast of watery porridge. As they were eating, there was a knock at the door. Honesty looked at his parents, wondering who it could be.

'Better open it then,' said Gran.

Outside was a man bundled in a coat and hat, with snowflakes dusting his clothes.

He nodded at Gran over Honesty's shoulder. 'Important message. From London. I was sent to tell you.'

'What message?' asked Honesty. They didn't even know anyone in London.

'Christmas. There's been a mistake.'

Mum and Dad had come to the door to listen.

'That law,' said the messenger. 'It shouldn't have said Christmas was *forbidden*. They wrote it down wrong. It should have said Christmas was *for giving*.'

'For *giving*? What does that mean?' asked Mum.

'For giving peace and goodwill to all men – that kind of thing.'

'You've ridden all the way from London to tell us that?' said Mum.

'All the way. That's the message. Merry Christmas!' The man doffed his hat and looked at Gran. Honesty saw her slip him a sixpence and he went off cheerfully, heading towards the tavern.

'Well!' said Mum, closing the door. 'I can't believe it!'

'Fancy Parliament making a mistake like that!' marvelled Dad.

'So it's all right?' said Honesty. 'We can have Christmas?'

They all looked at Mum, holding their breath.

She sighed wearily. 'Well, if it's the law, I suppose we'll have to.'

Honesty and his sisters let out a deafening cheer and danced around the room until they remembered that dancing was strictly forbidden.

Dad interrupted, 'Before you get too carried away, nothing's prepared. We haven't even bought a goose for dinner.'

'Or potatoes or plum pudding,' said Mum. 'All we've left in the pantry are a few mouldy turnips.'

Honesty's hopes were dashed as quickly as they'd risen. What sort of Christmas was it going to be without a proper Christmas dinner? Only Gran seemed unflustered.

'Oh, I shouldn't worry about that,' she said. 'It's Christmas – something will turn up.'

The snow fell steadily all morning, blanketing the streets with white. At eleven o'clock, there was a second knock at the door. This time Honesty rushed to open it. Outside stood Ratty Annie and her father.

'Are we too early?' she asked.

'Early for what?' asked Honesty.

'For Christmas dinner. We brought some mince pies and a nice big rat.' She held it up by its tail.

'Oh! Um . . . thanks. You'd better come in,' said Honesty. Ratty Annie stayed on the doorstep, winding a lock of dirty hair round her finger and looking rather awkward.

'I just wanted to say, you know, sorry – for calling your Gran a witch and all. Sorry.'

'It's Christmas. Come in and close the door before

117

we all freeze to death.' To Honesty's surprise it was Gran who had spoken.

After that visitors began to arrive thick and fast. Tom Turner and his wife were next to come, bringing a huge plum pudding and a jar of honey. The Brothertons and their six small children crowded into the house, bearing gifts of pies and cakes and dandelion wine. Best of all were the Swelters, who brought a plump pink goose bigger than a football, which they had towed to the house on a wooden sledge.

By five o'clock they were all squashed around the small table, sitting down to a Christmas feast. Grace was said and many toasts were raised to the cook. After dinner, Mercy and Patience took it in turns to stand on a chair and sing a carol.

'Well,' said Gran, catching Honesty's eye, 'I promised you a Christmas. Was it worth the wait?'

Honesty's eyes shone in the firelight. 'It's been the best Christmas day ever,' he said. 'Thanks, Gran.'

'Oh no, thanks to you,' said Gran. 'Look around – see what you did.'

Honesty looked at the happy faces around the table. Dad was pouring a glass of dandelion wine for

Mum, who was actually laughing. His sisters were tunnelling into the plum pudding with their spoons to see if they could find a sixpence. Across the table, Ratty Annie was whispering shyly in Jem Swelter's ear while Tom Turner was beaming at his wife. (The potions had taken a week to wear off but they both seemed back to their old selves, although Swelter often hummed to himself and couldn't see flowers without sniffing them.)

'But I still don't understand, Gran. How did you do it?' asked Honesty.

'Do what?'

'Save Christmas. Change the law.'

'Ahh.' Gran gave him a wink. 'That's my secret.'

Honesty stared at her, remembering the messenger at the door and Gran pressing a silver sixpence into his hand.

'You made it all up!' he burst out. 'The message from London – all of it. You made it up!'

Gran put a finger to her lips. 'Don't talk such nonsense! You think I go round telling lies? Now then, what about that present?'

'You've got me one?'

'I said I would, didn't I? Go and look under your bed.'

Honesty hurried off to look. He found a lumpy shape wrapped in a dirty cloth and tied with red ribbon. When he unwrapped it, he found a broomstick inside.

'Oh! Um . . . thanks,' he said, puzzled. 'But it's just a broom, isn't it? I mean, it doesn't . . ?'

'What – fly?' said Gran, widening her eyes. 'Really, child! Wherever do you get these ideas?'